Disney's

Winnie the Pooh's
CHRISTMAS STORIES

MOUSE WORKS

Santa Pooh, written by Nancy Parent, penciled by Lee Loetz, and painted by Brent Ford.

Stuck on Christmas, Santa's Little Helper, Merry Christmas, Winnie the Pooh!, and Eeyore's Christmas Surprise
adapted from stories by Bruce Talkington.

Stuck on Christmas, Santa's Little Helper, and Eeyore's Christmas Surprise
illustrated by John Kurtz.

Santa's Little Helper illustrated by Alvin S. White Studio.

The Night Before Christmas, Jingle Bells, and The Twelve Days of Christmas
illustrated by Sol Studios.

The Night Before Christmas based on the poem by Clement C. Moore.

Merry Christmas, Winnie the Pooh! illustrated by Alvin S. White Studio.

Find Mouse Works at www.DisneyBooks.com

Copyright © 1999 by Disney Enterprises, Inc.
Based on the Pooh stories by A. A. Milne.
Copyright © The Pooh Properties Trust.
Printed in the United States of America.
First Edition
1 3 5 7 9 10 8 6 4 2
ISBN: 0-7364-0109-1

Contents

✦ Santa Pooh ✦

This Christmas Eve while sitting
In my oh-so-thoughtful spot,
I had a thought while eating
From my tasty honeypot.

Perhaps I should play Santa Claus
For all my friends this year,
Dropping presents at their doorstep
And bringing Christmas cheer.

Tigger wants a bright red ball
That bounces up and down.
Eeyore needs a new pink bow
To wipe away his frown.

Rabbit wants new gardening tools
To help him sow and till.
Piglet needs more haycorns,
So that he can have his fill.

And everyone will *ooh* and *aah*
When they come to visit me,
'Cause there'll be so many presents
Underneath my Christmas tree!

★ Stuck on Christmas ★

Rabbit thought that Christmas was the most perfect time of the year. Of course, being Rabbit, he couldn't help trying to make it a bit *more* perfect.

He inspected his home. "These candles are dandy," he declared. "My tree is terrific. This stocking looks swell. And the squash I found looks just like a smiling Santa."

But Rabbit soon discovered that all was *not* quite as right as it seemed. His nose wrinkled and wriggled until . . . *"Achoo!"* Rabbit's chimney was full of sneezy soot!

Rabbit would soon fix that. From the bottom of his fireplace, he scrubbed and swept. Then he hopped to the top of his house, where he scoured and scraped.

Rabbit reached deeper into the chimney, trying to clean the hard-to-reach middle bit. He reached and reached until he was stuck!

Luckily, Pooh and Piglet were making a holiday visit. "Rabbit is stuck downside up!" cried Pooh.

So Piglet left to find friends who might help to unstick Rabbit.

When Piglet returned, he found Pooh was stuck in the chimney, too! "I thought I'd go up and get Rabbit," said Pooh. "But the chimney thought I'd stay here."

Tigger tried to whoosh them out by pumping a hand bellows.

As the soot flew, Rabbit's nose tickled and tingled until . . . *"ACHOO!"*
And down thumped Pooh and Rabbit. Grateful Rabbit made hot cocoa for everyone.

"A perfect Christmas doesn't come from dandy candles, swell stockings, smiling squashes, or even clean chimneys," he decided. "But from perfectly wonderful friends!"

★ The Night Before Christmas ★

'Twas the night before Christmas, when all through the house

Not a creature was stirring, not even a mouse;

The stockings were hung by the chimney with care,

In hopes that St. Nicholas soon would be there;

The children were nestled all snug in their beds,

While visions of sugarplums danced in their heads;

And Piglet in his kerchief, and I in my cap,

Had just settled our brains for a long winter's nap,

When out on the lawn there arose such a clatter,

I sprang from my bed to see what was the matter.

Away to the window I flew like a flash,

Tore open the shutters and threw up the sash.

When what to my wondering eyes should appear,

But a miniature sleigh and eight tiny reindeer,

With a little old driver, so lively and quick

I knew in a moment it must be St. Nick.

More rapid than eagles his
coursers they came,

And he whistled and shouted,
and called them by name:

"Now, Dasher! Now, Dancer!
Now, Prancer and Vixen!

On, Comet! On, Cupid! On,
Donder and Blitzen!

To the top of the porch,
to the top of the wall!

Now dash away, dash away,
dash away all!"

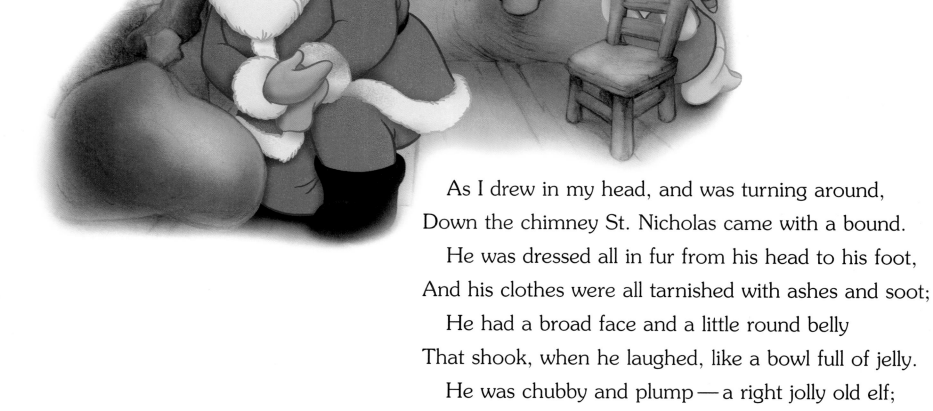

As I drew in my head, and was turning around,

Down the chimney St. Nicholas came with a bound.

He was dressed all in fur from his head to his foot,

And his clothes were all tarnished with ashes and soot;

He had a broad face and a little round belly

That shook, when he laughed, like a bowl full of jelly.

He was chubby and plump — a right jolly old elf;

And I laughed when I saw him, in spite of myself.

He spoke not a word, but went straight
to his work,
And filled all the stockings;
then turned with a jerk,
And laying his finger aside of his nose,
And giving a nod, up the chimney he rose.

He sprang to his sleigh, to his
team gave a whistle,
And away they all flew like the
down of a thistle;
But I heard him exclaim, ere he
drove out of sight,
"Happy Christmas to all,
and to all a good night!"

★ Eeyore's Christmas Surprise ★

One especially merry Christmas Eve, Eeyore decorated his house with shiny cranberries, boughs of evergreen, and a colorful wreath.

His friends all exclaimed that the little house had never looked better.

But when Eeyore pinned his yellow stocking to the front door, *CREAK* groaned the door! *RUMBLE* rattled the roof! *CRASH* went the house!

"It was too good to last," said Eeyore, sadly pulling his stocking from the pile.

"We can fix the place right up," said Rabbit. "It will just take some organizing."

"And some digging," added Gopher, making holes to hold the beams.

"And some sweeping," chimed in Piglet, cleaning up the new floor.

"And some helping!" shouted all of Eeyore's friends. Everyone rushed to rebuild the house — for how could Santa bring presents, if there was no home to bring them to?

But despite the organizing, digging, sweeping, and helping, Eeyore's house was not finished until after the sun rose on Christmas morning. Had Eeyore missed Christmas?

A glint of yellow caught his eye. It was his stocking, stuffed with gifts for everyone! "I guess Christmas comes wherever there's the Christmas spirit," said Eeyore.

All his friends in the Hundred-Acre Wood cheered. They knew he was right.

★ Jingle Bells ★

Dashing through the snow,
In a one-horse open sleigh,

O'er the fields we go,
Laughing all the way!

Bells on bobtails ring,
Making spirits bright,

What fun it is to ride and sing
A sleighing song tonight!

Jingle bells! Jingle bells!
Jingle all the way!
Oh, what fun it is to ride
In a one-horse open sleigh!

★ Santa's Little Helper ★

On the night before Christmas, Winnie the Pooh couldn't sleep. A growly grumble in his tummy urged him out of his bed and into his kitchen.

"Oh, bother," said Pooh. His kitchen was full of dirty pans and pots, but empty of the smallest sweet smackerel.

Then Pooh recalled that this was a "baking cookies for Santa" kind of mess! He hurried toward the fireplace, where he had left the treats. "Surely Santa would share a crumb or two to help a bear's rumbly tumbly," he quickly decided.

Before long, Santa had shared *every* crumb of *every* cookie with Pooh. With the plate empty, and his tummy quiet, at least for now, Pooh fell fast asleep.

He hadn't been dozing long, when a jolly voice rang out, "Merry Christmas!" Pooh awoke looking right into the twinkling eyes and smiling face of Santa Claus!

"I need your help, Pooh!" cried Santa. "Your friends have worked hard making treats for me, but I can't eat another bite." Santa didn't want anyone to think that he didn't like their gifts. So he asked Pooh, "Would you come with me and eat the snacks?"

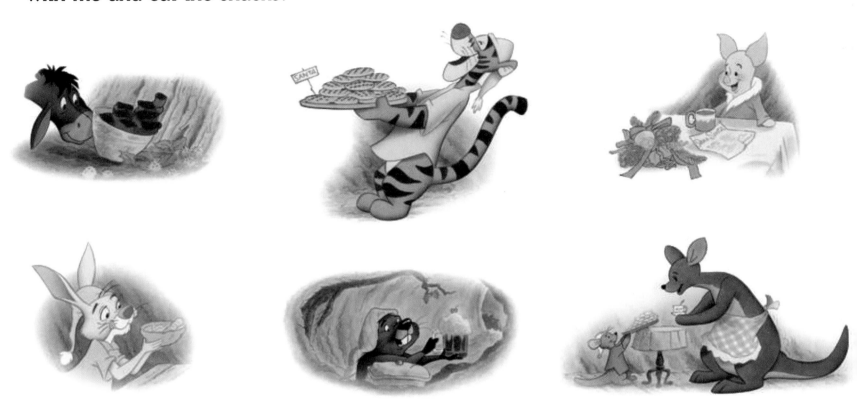

Pooh agreed, smiling a smile as large as his appetite! And in every home in the Hundred-Acre Wood, Santa left presents and Pooh left only the tiniest crumbs. Pooh did such a good job that Santa took him along for the rest of his visits!

Pooh munched his way around the world, finally falling fast asleep in Santa's sleigh.

Waking the next morning, Pooh saw that his kitchen was crammed with treats from all over the world. It was a wonderful Christmas present, but Pooh knew that the best gift was his adventure with Santa. "A happy memory never wears out or needs to be filled up again," said Pooh, smiling, "unlike a bear's rumbly tumbly!"

★ The Twelve Days of Christmas ★

On the twelfth day of Christmas
Christopher Robin sent to me

12

Twelve honeybees buzzing

11

Eleven pine trees swaying

10

Ten snowflakes falling

9

Nine jingle bells jingling

8

Eight wreaths for bouncing

7

Seven stockings for hanging

6

Six cards for mailing

5

FIVE POTS OF HONEY

4

3

Four carrots from Rabbit

Three thistles from Eeyore

2

1

Two Kanga-roos

and a Piglet in a pear tree.

Merry Christmas, Winnie the Pooh!

One snowy Christmas Eve, Winnie the Pooh looked up and down, in and out, and all around his house.

"I have a tree, some candles, and lots of decorations,"
he said, "but *something* seems to be missing."

Rap-a-tap-tap! A sudden small knocking made Pooh think that whatever was missing might be just outside his door.

But when Pooh opened the door, a small snowman stood shaking on his step.

"H-Hello, P-Pooh," said the snowman in a shivery, quivery, but oh-so-familiar voice. "The only thing I don't like about Christmas is that my ears get so very cold."

After much melting by Pooh's cozy fireplace, the snowman looked less like a snowman and more like Piglet!

"My!" said Pooh, happy to see a friend where there used to be a snowman.

"My!" said Piglet, now warm enough to see Pooh's glowing Christmas tree.

"Are you going to string popcorn for your tree?" asked Piglet.

"There *was* popcorn and string," admitted Pooh. "But now there's only string."

Piglet laughed. "Then we can use the string to wrap the presents you're giving."

Something began to tickle at the brain of the little bear. "I forgot to get presents!" exclaimed Pooh.

"Don't worry, Pooh," said Piglet, trying to smile bravely. "It's the thought that counts." Soon Piglet left to wrap his own presents.

Pooh didn't know what to do about the forgotten presents, but he did know where to find help.

"Hello!" called Pooh, knocking on Christopher Robin's door.

"Come in, Pooh," said Christopher Robin, smiling. "Why do you look sad on the most wonderful night of the year?"

But Pooh had forgotten all about the presents, again. "What are those?" he asked, pointing to some stockings hung by the fireplace.

"Those are stockings to hold Christmas presents," explained Christopher Robin. Poor Pooh suddenly remembered that he didn't have presents—or stockings.

Luckily the bear of little brain was smart enough to have a good friend. Christopher Robin gave Pooh stockings for himself and all of his friends.

Pooh thanked Christopher Robin and hurried off to deliver the stockings. "I will get everyone presents later," Pooh said to himself. "The stockings come first."

With a small note that said
"From Pooh," he left a stocking for

Piglet,

Tigger,

Rabbit,

Eeyore,

Gopher,

and Owl.

Back at his own comfy house, Pooh decided, "Now I must think about presents for my friends." But sleepy Pooh's thinking soon turned into dreaming.

Thump-a-bump-bump! The next morning, Pooh was awakened by a big and bouncy knock at his door. "Merry Christmas, Pooh!" shouted his friends.

Pooh opened the door. He was about to apologize for not having any presents to give when Piglet, Tigger, Rabbit, Gopher, Eeyore, and Owl started *thanking* him.

"No more cold ears with my new stocking cap," said Piglet.

"My stripedy sleeping bag is tigger-ific!" exclaimed Tigger.

"So is my new carrot cover," chimed in Rabbit.

Gopher thanked Pooh for the rock-collecting bag. Eeyore happily swished his toasty tail-warmer.

And Owl announced that his wind sock was just the thing to let him know which way the breeze was blowing.

"Something awfully nice is going on," said Pooh. "But I'm not sure how it happened."

"It's called Christmas, buddy bear," replied Tigger. Then everyone gave presents to Pooh: lots of pots of honey.

Surrounded by his friends and his favorite tasty treats, Pooh had
to agree. "Christmas! What a sweet thought, indeed."